Wild Colt

Lois Szymanski
Illustration by Linda Kantjas

4880 Lower Valley Road • Atglen, PA • 19310

Designed by *Danielle D. Farmer*
Cover Design by *Bruce M. Waters*
Type set in AdineKirnberg/Angsana New

ISBN: 978-0-7643-3975-2
Printed in China

Schiffer Books are available at special discounts for bulk purchases for sales promotions or premiums. Special editions, including personalized covers, corporate imprints, and excerpts can be created in large quantities for special needs. For more information contact the publisher:

Published by Schiffer Publishing Ltd.
4880 Lower Valley Road
Atglen, PA 19310
Phone: (610) 593-1777; Fax: (610) 593-2002
E-mail: Info@schifferbooks.com

For the largest selection of fine reference books on this and related subjects, please visit our website at **www.schifferbooks.com**
We are always looking for people to write books on new and related subjects. If you have an idea for a book, please contact us at **proposals@schifferbooks.com**

This book may be purchased from the publisher.
Include $5.00 for shipping.
Please try your bookstore first.
You may write for a free catalog.

In Europe, Schiffer books are distributed by
Bushwood Books
6 Marksbury Ave.
Kew Gardens
Surrey TW9 4JF England
Phone: 44 (0) 20 8392 8585; Fax: 44 (0) 20 8392 9876
E-mail: info@bushwoodbooks.co.uk
Website: www.bushwoodbooks.co.uk

Other Schiffer Books By The Author:
Grandfather's Secret, 978-0-7643-3535-8, $12.99
The True Story of Seafeather, 978-0-7643-3609-6, $14.99
Out of the Sea, Today's Chincoteague Pony, 978-0-87033-595-2, $14.95

Other Schiffer Books on Related Subjects:
Once a Pony Time at Chincoteague, 978-0-87033-436-8, $9.95
Majesty from Assateague, 978-0-87033-552-5, $8.95

Dedication

For Katelynn Donaldson, who is always a winner in my book. –LS

To Cate and Will Misczuk, because I care. –LK

Still and warm
Quiet night
Whooshing, sliding
Sudden bright

Wet and blinking
Crooked ear
Whuffing, touching
Mama's near

Nudging soft
"Son, come stand."
Wobbling, falling
Scratchy sand

Rooting, finding
Milk so warm
Tail is switching
Flies that swarm

By the creek,
Moving sand,
One ghost crab,
Waving hand

Tails in front,
Foal behind,

Moving forward

In a line

Warm and breezy

Mosquitoes buzz

Eggshells crackle

Duckling fuzz!

Deer with fawn
At water hole
Turtles float,
Eyeing foal

Ocean salty
Foals race surf
Sandy beaches
Bucking turf

Thunder booms!
Lightning flash!
Sky grows dark,
Sea waves crash

White moon rising
Raccoon night
Dark and snarling
Foxes fight

Eyes wide open
Colt huddles close
Shivering, touching
Momma's nose

Long, lazy,
Grazy days
Colt grows tall
Summer haze

One hot morning
One loud shout
Men on horses
All about

Whooping, swooping
Cowboys cry
Herd trots out,
Heads held high

To the bay
To the ledge
Plunging deep
From the edge

Between the boats
Toward the crowd
Swimming forward
Crowds shout loud

Clomp, clomp,
clomp…
Kids line streets
Ponies press
Cowboys keep

Crabcakes, popcorn
Smell the air
Cotton candy
Country fair

Away from herd

Mare draws close

"Goodbye, son."

Touch of nose

Cowboy leads
Colt bucks high
Doesn't want
To say goodbye

Auctioneer calls
Folks gather round
Numbers yelled
Gavel down!

Sold to the girl
In the ball cap
"My colt," she shouts
Crowds start to clap

Hugging close

Soft child's tone

Colt draws close

Going home

Can you find these wetlands creatures in the story?

Drake Mallard Duck

American Oystercatcher

Little Blue Heron

Great Blue Heron

White Tailed Deer

Glossy Ibis

Painted Turtle

Flicker

King Fisher

Herring Gull

Cattle Egret

Sanderling

Ghost Crab

Bald Eagle

Hen Mallard Duck

Raccoon

Sika Deer

Red Fox

Red Winged Blackbird

Eastern Cottontail

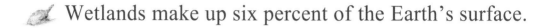

Facts About Wetlands

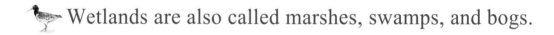

Wetlands make up six percent of the Earth's surface.

Wetlands are also called marshes, swamps, and bogs.

Wetlands exist in all regions of the United States.

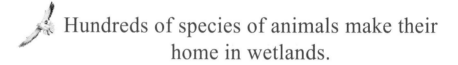

Hundreds of species of animals make their home in wetlands.

Wetlands are not wet all year round.

Wetlands can contain fresh water, salt water, or brackish water, a combination of both.

Discussion Topics

What is a symbiotic relationship?

What is brackish water?

What plant species reside in the Assateague wetlands?

What are wetlands?